This edition published by Parragon in 2009
Parragon
Queen Street House
4 Queen Street
Bath BA1 1HE, UK

ISBN 978-1-4075-8190-3

Printed in China

Disney
Sleeping Beauty
a Moment to Remember

By Catherine McCafferty • Illustrated by the Disney Storybook Artists

PaRragon

Bath · New York · Singapore · Hong Kong · Cologne · Delhi · Melbourne

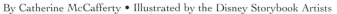

$\mathscr{P}$rincess Aurora sighed. Life in the palace was so very different from the quiet glade where she had met Prince Phillip. That night there would be yet another royal ball and the fairies were arguing over what she should wear.

"Now, dears," said Flora, "we all know that this outfit suits Aurora best. Don't you think so, Aurora?"

Before Aurora could answer them, Prince Phillip came into the room.

"Hello, dearest," he said.

"Oh, Phillip, I'm so glad to see you. I - " Aurora began.

"Ahem," the royal florist interrupted. "Princess Aurora, could you please tell the royal table setter that she must place flowers in the middle of each table tonight?"

"And could you please tell the royal florist that our guests won't see one another if I put his big flower arrangements on the tables?" said the royal table setter.

"Let's put just one flower on each table," Aurora suggested.

"A single flower?" muttered the servants. "The guests will be insulted!"

"You were saying, dear?" Phillip asked.

"Pardon me, Princess," said the royal steward, "but you must approve the seating arrangements."

"Thank you, Steward," said Aurora. "I will look at them - "

"When we return," Prince Phillip finished. He took the surprised princess's hand. "We're going out where no one can ask us anything."

As they mounted their horses, Phillip turned to Aurora. "I'm sorry, I forgot that the Royal Guard must come with us."

Aurora looked at the ten riders behind them and tried to hide her disappointment. Then she leaned down and whispered to Phillip's horse. Samson charged away from the palace with Aurora's horse following him. Soon, the Royal Guard was far behind.

"Whoa, Samson!" Phillip shouted. But the horse galloped deep into the forest. Then Samson stopped suddenly.

Splash! Phillip sailed over Samson's head and landed in a stream.

"No carrots for you, boy!" Prince Phillip scolded his horse. He looked up and saw Aurora trying to hide a giggle.

"Do you remember this place, Phillip?" Aurora asked.

Phillip climbed out of the stream. He pulled off his boots and emptied the water out of them.

Aurora took off her shoes, too. She spun around gracefully, humming a tune.

"Yes," Prince Phillip said softly. "I remember this place. . . ."

"I will never forget that day," said Aurora, "no matter how crowded our lives become with royal duties."

Prince Phillip smiled. "Nor will I," he told her.

Phillip and Aurora held hands, wishing they could bring the peace and love they knew in the glade back to the palace.

Their peaceful moment ended as the Royal Guard thundered into the glade.

Phillip put on his hat and cape. Then he handed Aurora a single flower.

Aurora took the gift and smiled. "We should go back and get ready for the ball," she said.

"You go ahead, dear," Phillip said. "I'll be back soon."

As she rode off, Aurora decided to plan a special surprise for the prince.

Meanwhile, Phillip had a surprise of his own.

"Not a word of this to the princess," he said to her animal friends as he gathered some flowers.

For the rest of the afternoon, Princess Aurora worked on Phillip's surprise. Flora, Fauna, and Merryweather flitted about, helping wherever they could.

More than once, Aurora heard a servant murmur, "Our guests will certainly be . . . surprised."

Aurora just smiled. "It is Prince Phillip I want to surprise," she said. "Not a word of this to him."

That night, after the fairies had helped Aurora into her gown, Prince Phillip came into the room. He held out a simple crown made from the flowers of the glade. "Would you like to wear this, too?" he asked.

"Oh, Phillip!" Aurora cried as she put on the crown and hugged her husband. "It is perfect for this evening."

Aurora led Phillip down the stairs to the ballroom. "Now I have a surprise for *you*!" The ballroom was dark and empty.

"You've cancelled the ball?" Prince Phillip asked.

"No, Phillip," Aurora answered. "You brought a bit of our little glade to me in this beautiful crown. Now let me take you back to our glade."

A sweet breeze blew through the flowers and trees in the ballroom's courtyard. Water danced in the fountain. Candles flickered in the darkness.

"The glade will always be in our hearts," Aurora whispered. "But now it is in our palace, too."

Just then, Phillip's father, King Hubert, approached.

"This is much better than the stuffy balls I usually attend," he said to Princess Aurora. "Thank you, my dear!"

And as Aurora and Phillip danced, their little friends added their own magic from the glade.